Bad Bear Detectives

An **IRVING & MUKTUK** Story

DANIEL PINKWATER
Illustrated by JILL PINKWATER

Houghton Mifflin Company 2006

For Valerie and Ken,
good friends who make
our garden grow.

www.houghtonmifflinbooks.com

The text of this book is set in Leawood.
The illustrations were created with felt-
tip marker and ink on Bristol board.

*Library of Congress Cataloging-in-
Publication Data*

Pinkwater, Daniel Manus, 1941–
Bad bear detectives / by Daniel
Pinkwater ; illustrated by Jill Pinkwater.
p. cm.
Summary: Irving and Muktuk,
polar bears at the zoo in Bayonne,
New Jersey, are the natural suspects
when someone steals a shipment of
imported muffins, but they decide to
prove that they are not bad bears by
finding the real thief.
ISBN 0-618-43125-X (hc)
[1. Polar bears—Fiction. 2.
Bears—Fiction. 3. Stealing—
Fiction. 4. Muffins—Fiction. 5.
Humorous stories.] I. Pinkwater,
Jill, ill. II. Title.
PZ7.P6335Bab 2006
[E]—dc22

2004018780

ISBN-13: 978-0618-43125-0

Manufactured in China
SCP 10 9 8 7 6 5 4 3 2 1

Captain Hare

A news item appears in the *Bayonne Tribune:*

Bayonne
Tribune

Dirty Work on the Docks

Last night, a large shipment of expensive Italian designer muffins disappeared from a waterfront warehouse. The muffins had been unloaded from the ship *Gorgonzola Maru* earlier in the day. This morning, the muffins were gone. Bayonne City Police found only one clue—a large fat footprint.

"This could be the work of bears," Police Captain Hare told our reporter.

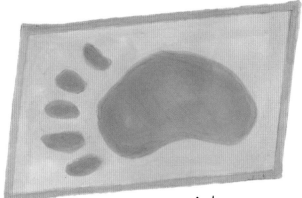

Large fat footprint

In their quarters at the Bayonne Zoo, Irving and Muktuk, each a bad bear if there ever was one, are cheating each other at cards.

The door bursts open, and Captain Hare runs in. With him are Mr. Goldberg, the bear keeper, the Zoo Director, and two policemen.

"Paws up!" Captain Hare says. "You are suspected!"

"We did nothing!" Irving and Muktuk say. "We are innocent."

"Banana oil!" says Captain Hare. "Your weakness for muffins is well known, and this time you have gone too far."

Irving and Muktuk begin to cry. "Tell him we are innocent," they say to the Zoo Director.

"They are not to be trusted," the Zoo Director says. "If it is proven that they took the muffins, they will be locked in their room at night, and they will have to pick up trash around the zoo for a year."

"But we did nothing," Irving and Muktuk say.

"Fish cakes!" Captain Hare says. "We will take sweepings of muffin crumbs from this room and study them in the police laboratory. If we find a single Italian blueberry, I will cart you off to the slammer."

"The slammer?" Irving and Muktuk ask through their tears.

"I have thrown plenty of polar bears in jail," Captain Hare says.

"Really? Polar bears?"

"Well, bears, anyway," Captain Hare says. "When we get the evidence, you will get what you deserve."

"We didn't do it," Irving and Muktuk say.

"Birdseed! The Law has its eye on you," Captain Hare says.

Captain Hare, Mr. Goldberg, the Zoo Director, and the police officers leave Irving and Muktuk alone.

"This is bad," Muktuk says. "Make one mistake, and anytime a muffin goes missing, the coppers are all over you."

"It is unfair," Irving says.

"Of course, we have made more than one mistake," Muktuk says.

"That is true," Irving says. "Remember the time we snuck into the muffin factory?"

"Yes," Muktuk says.

"That was a good one," Irving says.

"Yes," Muktuk says.

Irving and Muktuk drool, thinking about their past crimes.

"But this time it is different," Muktuk says. "We are falsely accused. There is only one thing to do."

"Yes! Run away!" Irving says.

"No!" Muktuk says. "We must find out who really took the muffins. We must remove this smirch from our names."

"Our names are smirched?" Irving asks.

"Badly smirched," Muktuk says. "People think we are bad bears. They think we are not to be trusted."

"We are bad bears," Irving says. "We are not to be trusted."

"Do you want to be locked in at night and have to pick up trash for a year?" Muktuk asks.

"We must find the one who stole the muffins!" Irving says.

"We will be detectives."

"First we must steal hats," Muktuk says.

"Hats?" Irving asks.

"All detectives have hats," Muktuk says. "The Zoo Director has hats. We will take two of hers."

"Isn't it a bad idea, when we are going to prove we did not steal something, to start out by stealing hats?" Irving asks.

"We have no choice," Muktuk says. "Without hats, we would be spotted as polar bears in a minute."

Later that night, wearing hats, Irving and Muktuk sneak out of the zoo.

"What do we do now?" Irving asks.

"We go to the scene of the crime," Muktuk says. "We sniff around. We look for clues. We ask questions."

"Is a clue like a muffin?" Irving asks.

"Yes," Muktuk says. "A muffin would be a good clue."

"Do detectives ever eat clues?" Irving asks.

"Sometimes," Muktuk says.

The Bayonne docks are deserted. Irving and Muktuk see a night watchman making his rounds.

"I will be the good detective. You be the bad detective," Muktuk says.

"OK. I will be bad," Irving says.

"Hey, watchman!" Muktuk says. "Tell us what you know, or my friend will eat your lunch."

"Grrr!" Irving growls.

"I know nothing," the night watchman says.

"What do you know about the large shipment of muffins that was stolen?"
Muktuk asks the night watchman.

"I know nothing," the night watchman says.

"Grrr!" Irving growls.

"What did you see? What did you hear?" Irving asks.

"I saw nothing. I heard nothing. I know nothing," the night watchman says.

"Nothing?" Muktuk asks.

"Nothing."

"Do we eat his lunch now?" Irving asks.

"No," Muktuk says. "We look for clues."

"Is this a clue?" Irving asks.

"Yes!" Muktuk says. "It is a footprint! Footprints are excellent clues."

"It's a large fat footprint," Irving says. "This could be the work of bears."

"It is a large fat footprint," Muktuk says. "It could be the footprint of a bear, and do you know why?"

"Why?" Irving asks.

"Because that is your footprint, you silly polar bear!" Muktuk says.

"No, it isn't," Irving says. "Here are my footprints, under my feet. This is a footprint I found. It is a clue."

"If that is so . . . " Muktuk says.

"Then the one who took the muffins could be a bear," Irving says.

"Now we are making progress," Muktuk says.

"If you were a bear . . ." Muktuk says.
"I am a bear," Irving says.
"If you were a bear, and you took the muffins, what would you do next?" Muktuk asks.

"I would eat them!" Irving says.

"What if there were too many muffins to eat all at once?" Muktuk asks. "What would you do then?"

"I would give some to you," Irving says.

"What if there were too many muffins for both of us to eat?" Muktuk asks.

"That would be a lot of muffins," Irving says.

"What would you do?" Muktuk asks.

"I would hide them," Irving says. "I would hide them and come back and eat them later."

"Exactly," Muktuk says. "So, all we have to do is find where this bear hid the muffins."

"And then we eat them," Irving says.

"Then we wait for the bear to come back," Muktuk says.

"I'm hungry," Irving says.

"Now to find where this bear hid the muffins," Muktuk says.
"How do we do that?" Irving asks.
"We are polar bears!" Muktuk says.
"You're right! We are!" Irving says.
"And what are polar bears best at?" Muktuk asks.
"Swimming!" Irving says.

"And what else are polar bears good at?" Muktuk asks.

"Eating?"

"Yes, and are polar bears good at anything else?" Muktuk asks.

"Being very large?"

"Polar bears are good at sniffing!" Muktuk says. "As polar bears we can sniff things from miles away."

"I knew that!" Irving says. "I am a good sniffer."

"You have the finest nose of any polar bear I have ever seen," Muktuk says. "You can find the muffins."

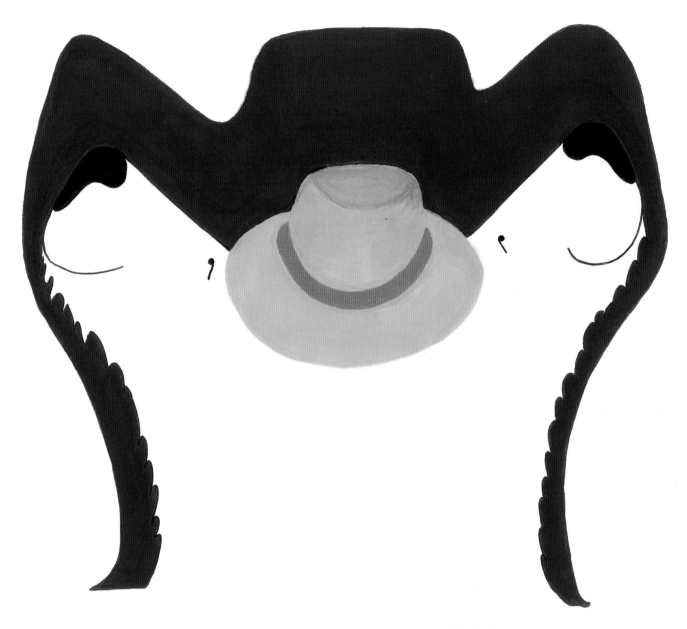

Irving lifts his great nose into the air. First he sniffs left.
Then he sniffs right. Then he sniffs left again.

"I smell crumbs!" Irving says.

"Muffin crumbs?" Muktuk asks.

"Muffin crumbs!" Irving says.

"Which way?"

"This way!"

Irving follows his nose, and Muktuk follows Irving.

"What are you smelling now?" Muktuk asks.

"They are very high quality muffins," Irving says.

"I can smell them, too!" Muktuk says.

"Can you smell the blueberries?" Irving asks.

"No! Are there blueberries?" Muktuk asks.

"They seem to be *mirtilli dell'Italia,* or blueberries of Italy,"
Irving says. "And I am sniffing something else."

"What?" Muktuk asks.

"Bear!" Irving says.

"So it is a bear!" Muktuk says.

"Two bears," Irving says. "They smell quite smart."

"What a nose!" Muktuk says. "You can smell that they are smart?"

"These are the smartest smelling bears I have ever sniffed," Irving says.

"The smart bears went up this street,"
Irving says.
Irving runs up the street. Muktuk follows.

"The smart bears made a right turn here," Irving says.
Irving turns right. Muktuk turns right.

"Red light! Stop for the red light," Irving says.
Irving and Muktuk wait for the light to change.
"Green light! Follow the smart bears!" Irving says.

"We're getting close," Irving says. "The muffin scent is strong."
"We're near the zoo," Muktuk says.
"We're very near," Irving says.
"We're in the zoo!" Muktuk says.

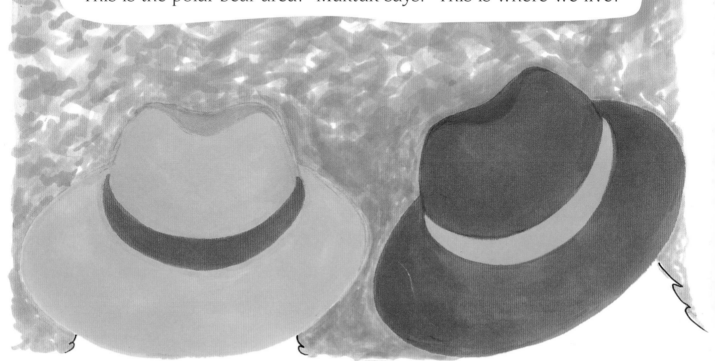

In the polar bear area, next to the polar bear pool, there is a waterfall. Behind the waterfall there is a small space, like a little cave. Irving leads Muktuk behind the waterfall.

"The muffins!" Muktuk says.

There are the stolen muffins, slightly soggy.

"So, the smart bears brought the muffins here!" Irving says. "Have one—they're good!"

Irving and Muktuk eat muffins.

ITALIA

ITALIA

"You know, these muffins remind me of something," Muktuk says.

"Yes, they taste familiar to me, too," Irving says.

"I'm getting a mental picture," Muktuk says.

"So am I," Irving says.

"I seem to remember that we took these muffins from someplace," Muktuk says.

"It was a warehouse. It was the warehouse down on the waterfront," Irving says, chewing.

"So, it *was* us! We did take the muffins!" Muktuk says.

"We will be locked in our room at night," Muktuk says.
"And we will have to pick up trash around the zoo for a year," Irving says.
"Well . . ." Muktuk says.
"Well . . ." Irving says.
"A year is not such a long time. Have another muffin."